For Charlie Everton Bingham

CIP Data is available.

First published in the United States 1993 by
Dutton Children's Books, a division of Penguin Books USA Inc.
375 Hudson Street, New York, New York 10014

Originally published in Great Britain 1992 by
Hutchinson Children's Books, a division of Random Century, London

Printed in Hong Kong   First American Edition
10 9 8 7 6 5 4 3 2 1
ISBN 0-525-44991-4

A Fox
Got My Socks

HILDA OFFEN

Dutton Children's Books • *New York*

On a sunny washing day,

Pretend to wash clothes.

my clothes flip-flapped
and blew away.

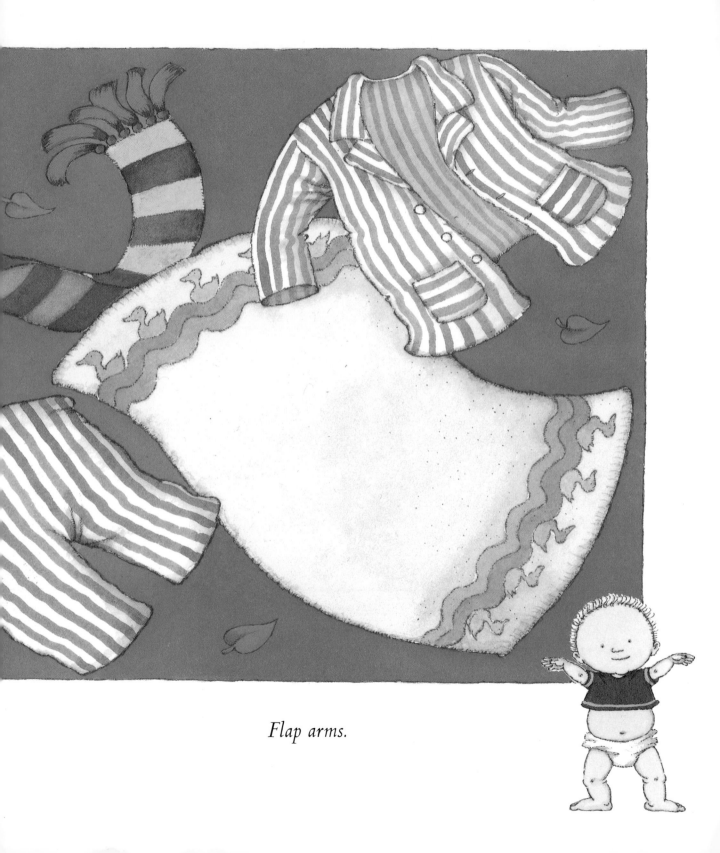

Flap arms.

A cat got my hat.

Touch head with both hands.

A fox got my socks.

Touch feet.

A goat got my coat.

Pretend to fasten buttons.

An owl got my towel.

Pretend to flap towel.

"Oh no!" said the pig.
"These pants are too big!"

Pretend to hold up pants.

And the bear gave a snort:
"This sweater's too short!"

Pull up sweater.

Two baby llamas
were in my pajamas.

Pretend to touch pajama top and bottom.

My scarf made me laugh,
wrapped around a giraffe.

Pretend to wrap scarf around your neck.

But the sun was so hot,

Fan face.

I said, "Keep what you've got."   *Hold out arms.*

"Because...

...I'm happy enough
without all that stuff!"

Dance around.